ALBERT IS JUST FINE, MRS. EINSTEIN!

By MICHAEL DAHL

Illustrated by FABIO LEONE

CANTATA LEARNING
MANKATO, MINNESOTA

CANTATA LEARNING
MANKATO, MINNESOTA

Published by Cantata Learning
1710 Roe Crest Drive
North Mankato, MN 56003
www.cantatalearning.com

Copyright © 2015 Cantata Learning

All rights reserved. No part of this publication may be reproduced
in any form without written permission from the publisher.

Library of Congress Control Number: 2014938270
978-1-63290-083-8 (hardcover/CD)
978-1-63290-163-7 (paperback/CD)
978-1-63290-398-3 (paperback)

Albert Is Just Fine, Mrs. Einstein! by Michael Dahl
Illustrated by Fabio Leone

Book design by Tim Palin Creative
Music produced by Wes Schuck
Audio recorded, mixed, and mastered at Two Fish Studios, Mankato, MN

Printed in the United States of America.

WWW.CANTATALEARNING.COM/ACCESS-OUR-MUSIC

Albert Einstein is known as one of the greatest **scientists** of all time. His ideas changed how people think about the world and even the universe. When he was young, people thought that Einstein was not very smart, and that he would never do well in school. Einstein overcame many challenges and is a role model for people today.

"Poor Albert!" says his Mother,
"He's **timid**, and he's shy.
And fast and busy children
always push him and pass him by."

"Poor Albert!" says his mother.

"He's slow at reading too.

He's slow with books and numbers.

What can a mother do?"

Don't worry, Mrs. Einstein,
your Albert is a brain.
He's quiet on the outside,
because he's busy on the inside.
Your Albert is just fine.
Your Albert is just fine.

Inside he's always thinking about space and shining stars.

He thinks about bikes and railroad cars.

We think that Albert will go far!

Don't worry, Mrs. Einstein.

Your Albert will go far.

"Poor Albert," says his mother.
"He's slow at talking too.
He never said a single word
'til after he was two."

"Poor Albert," says his mother.

"He likes to stare at trains.

He stares at rocks and clicking clocks.

He hasn't got a brain!"

Don't worry, Mrs. Einstein,

your Albert is a brain.

He's quiet on the outside,

because he's busy on the inside.

Your Albert is just fine.

Your Albert is just fine.

Inside he's always thinking about space and shining stars.

He thinks about bikes and railroad cars.

We think that Albert will go far!

Don't worry, Mrs. Einstein.

Your Albert will go far.

GLOSSARY

scientist—a person who studies the world around us

timid—to be shy and afraid

universe—everything that exists, including the Earth, the planets, the stars, and all of space

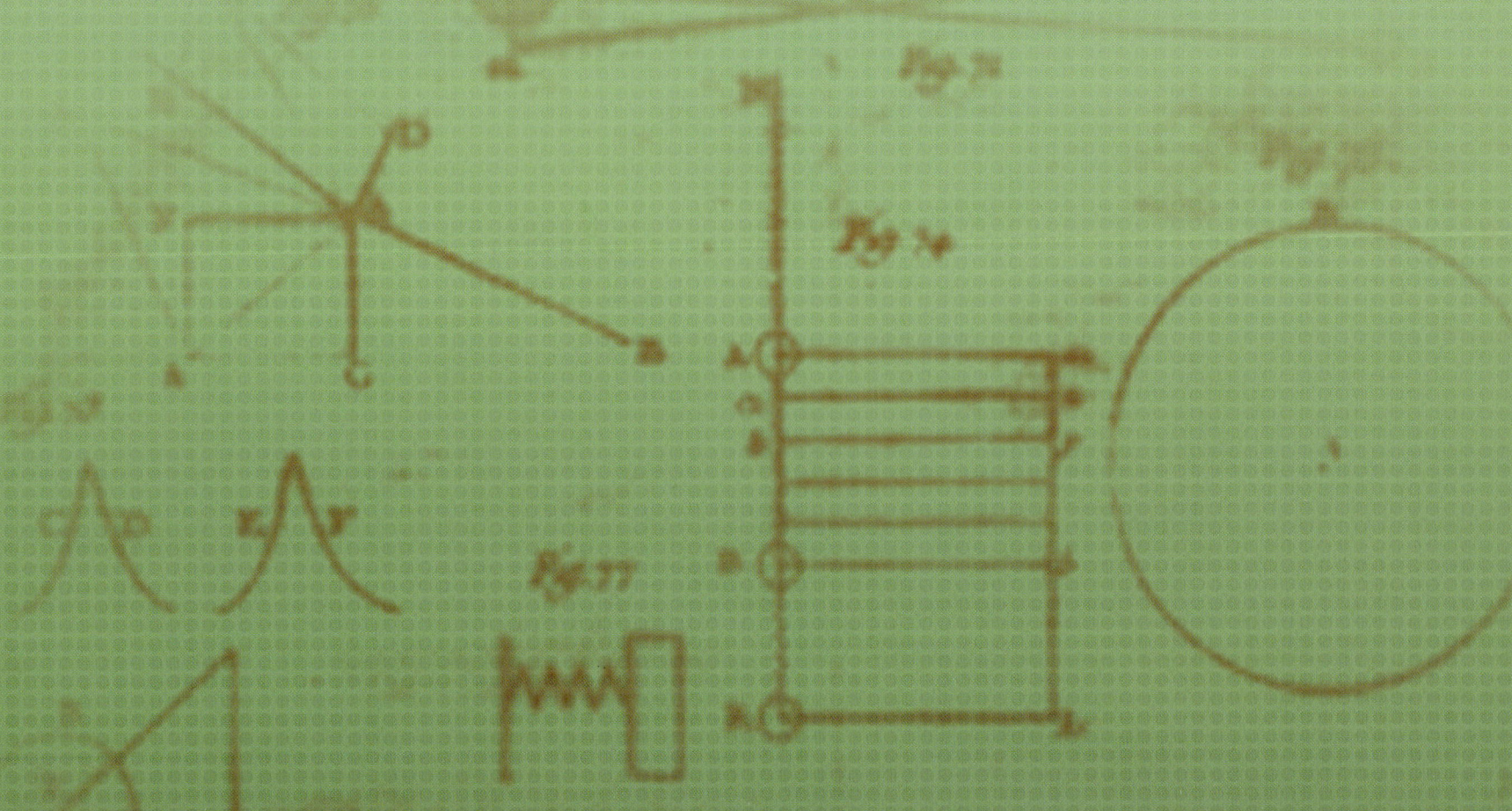

Albert Is Just Fine, Mrs. Einstein

Michael Dahl
Alternative Rock

Online music access and CDs available at www.cantatalearning.com

TO LEARN MORE

Berne, Jennifer. *On a Beam of Light: A Story of Albert Einstein.* San Francisco: Chronicle Books, 2013.

Brallier, Jess. *Who Was Albert Einstein?* New York: Grosset and Dunlap, 2002.

Pohlen, Jerome. *Albert Einstein and Relativity for Kids.* Chicago: Chicago Review Press, 2012.

Slade, Suzanne. *Albert Einstein: Scientist and Genius.* Minneapolis, MN: Picture Window Books, 2008.